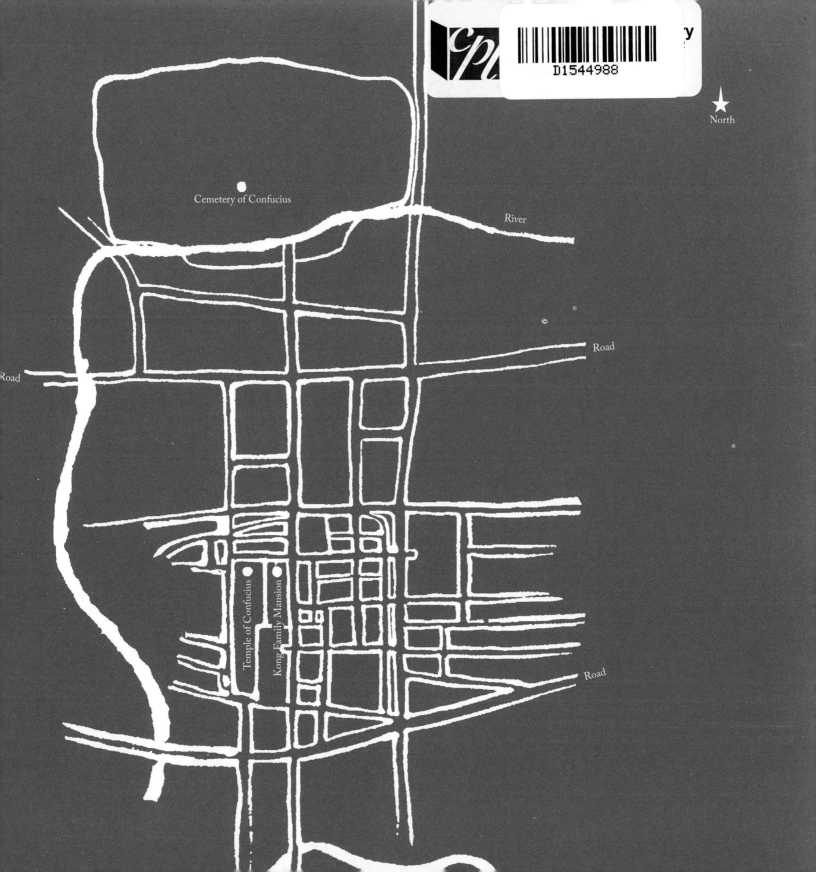

North

Cemetery of Confucius

River

Road

Road

Temple of Confucius

Kong Family Mansion

Road

Road

Ming's Adventure with
Confucius in Qufu

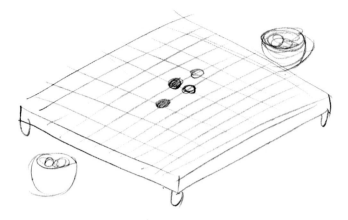

This book is edited and designed by the Editorial Committee of *Cultural China* series.

Story and Illustrations: Li Jian
Translation: Yijin Wert

Editorial Assistant: Cao Xiaoying
Editors: Yang Xiaohe, Anna Nguyen
Editorial Director: Zhang Yicong

Senior Consultants: Sun Yong, Wu Ying, Yang Xinci
Managing Director and Publisher: Wang Youbu

ISBN: 978-1-60220-989-3

Address any comments about *Ming's Adventure with Confucius in Qufu* to:

Better Link Press
99 Park Ave
New York, NY 10016
USA

or

Shanghai Press and Publishing Development Company
F 7 Donghu Road, Shanghai, China (200031)
Email: comments_betterlinkpress@hotmail.com

Printed in China by Shanghai Donnelley Printing Co., Ltd.

1   3   5   7   9   10   8   6   4   2

曲阜孔庙、孔府和孔林

Ming's Adventure with
Confucius in Qufu

A Story in English and Chinese

by Li Jian
Translated by Yijin Wert

Better Link Press

After finding out that Ming was learning the teachings of Confucius or Master Kong in school, his parents decided to take him on a special trip to Qufu. It was the perfect place to introduce Ming to the philosopher's teachings.

小明正在学校里学习孔子和他的学说，于是爸爸妈妈特地带他去曲阜旅行。在曲阜为小明介绍这位哲学家的学说，最合适不过了。

Qufu is the hometown of Confucius, a small city with a 3,000-year-old history. There are three famous Confucian sites in Qufu.

曲阜是孔子的故乡，这个小城市有约3000年的历史。这里有著名的"三孔"。

The Temple of Confucius is the oldest set of buildings in Chinese history. It is a model of over 2,000 temples of Confucius found throughout China and overseas.

孔庙是中国历史最悠久的一组建筑物，也是海内外2000多座孔庙的范本。

The Kong Family Mansion was the home of many decedents of Confucius. The front part of the mansion was used as offices while the family lived in the back part of the mansion. To the north of the mansion, there was a garden.

孔府是孔子许多代后裔的家。大宅的前面办公，后面居住，它的北面有一个花园。

The Cemetery of Confucius is the burial place of Confucius and the final resting place of his descendants. The cemetery is surrounded by many precious ancient trees and plants. It is said that they were moved here from many different places by Confucius's students after his death.

孔林是孔子的墓地，他的子孙们也长眠于此。孔林有很多古老珍稀的植物。相传孔子去世后，弟子们将各地的奇木移植至此。

Ming and his family first visited
the Temple of Confucius.

小明一家先到孔庙游玩。

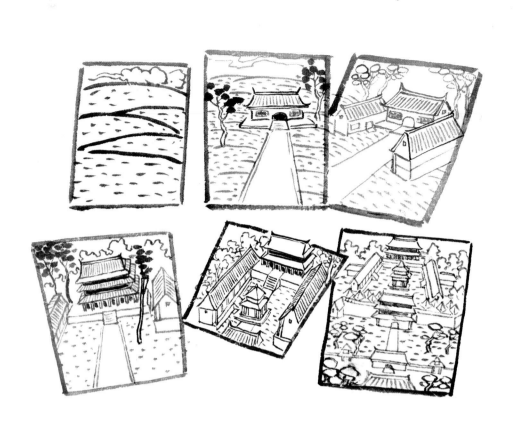

The Temple of Confucius was established at his residence in 478 BC, one year after Confucius's death. It was devoted to the memory of Confucius by his students. Ever since then, people have never stopped worshipping him. The temple has been expanded repeatedly over a period of more than 2,400 years.

孔子逝世的第二年即公元前478年，他的弟子们为纪念老师，在孔子的故居立庙纪念。2400余年间，人们从未停止纪念活动，孔庙在不断扩建。

It is believed that Confucius used to give his lectures in the Apricot Pavilion. He had over 3,000 students during his life-long teaching career.

孔子就是在杏坛所在的地方聚众讲学。在他的教育生涯中，收授的弟子超过3000人。

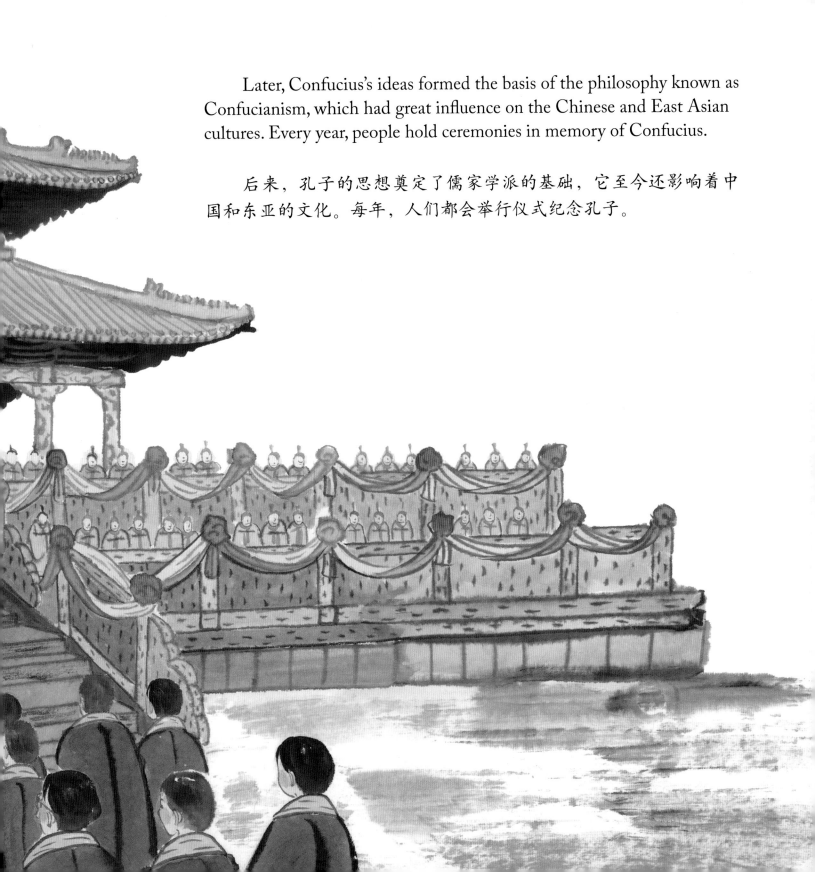

Later, Confucius's ideas formed the basis of the philosophy known as Confucianism, which had great influence on the Chinese and East Asian cultures. Every year, people hold ceremonies in memory of Confucius.

后来，孔子的思想奠定了儒家学派的基础，它至今还影响着中国和东亚的文化。每年，人们都会举行仪式纪念孔子。

Main Gate 大门

Chongguang Gate 重光门

Ming and his family left the temple and went to visit the Kong Family Mansion.

小明和爸爸妈妈离开了孔庙，继续参观孔府。

Mansion for living 后

Alley 巷道

Alley 巷道

Ming went into the garden. On a table in the pavilion, Ming noticed a very old go game set. He laid a go stone on the board. As he was doing so, something strange happened ...

小明走进了花园。在凉亭里的桌子上，小明发现了一副老旧的棋盘和棋子。他拿起一枚棋子放在棋盘上。就在此时，奇怪的事情发生了……

Suddenly, Ming found himself tumbling down a mysterious dark tunnel that led to a peaceful place with some humble looking houses and an old man.

"I am Confucius. Welcome to my home!" the old man greeted Ming with a smile.

突然，小明发现自己跌入了一个黑漆漆的隧道。隧道通向一个宁静的地方，这里有几间简陋的屋子和一位老者。
"我是孔丘，欢迎来我家！"老者笑眯眯地迎接小明。

Ming told Confucius that his philosophy was as popular as ever after over 2,400 years. Confucius and his students were thrilled to hear Ming's report from the future.

"I only know that you are one of the early teachers of the Golden Rule: 'What you do not wish for yourself, do not do to others.' Could you teach me more?" Ming continued.

Confucius gladly agreed. "My students and I will teach you the Six Arts as an introduction." In return, Ming offered to tell them more about his life.

小明告诉孔子，2400多年后的今天他的学说还在流传。听到这来自未来的消息，孔子和他的弟子们都很激动。

"我只知道您的一句名言'已所不欲勿施于人'，能再教我多些么？"小明说。

孔子高兴地同意了："我和弟子们先教你'六艺'。"作为感谢，小明答应要给他们讲更多自己的事。

Lesson One Rites
第一课 礼

Ming first learned how to greet other people.

首先，小明学习与人见面时的礼仪。

He showed them a handshake, considered a common greeting today.

小明跟他们握手，这是现在最常用的问候方式。

Lesson Two Music

第二课 乐

Then Confucius explained to Ming that the study of music
instills a sense of harmony in people.

然后孔子对小明说，学习音乐能让人们感受到和谐。

Ming talked about how people today enjoy music from instruments like the violin and trumpet.

小明介绍说，今天的人们如何欣赏小提琴和小号等乐器演奏出的音乐。

Lesson Three Archery
第三课 射

By practicing archery, people not only gained proficiency at war skills, but they also cultivated their minds, said Confucius.

孔子说，练习射箭不仅能提高作战水平，还能锻炼意志。

Ming then tried to explain how guns were eventually used in wars.

小明试着解释枪械如何在战争中使用。

Lesson Four Chariot-Driving
第四课 御

While working with a horse, Ming found out that becoming a charioteer required the combined use of intellect and physical strength.

试驾马车时，小明发现要成为一位驭手，需要兼备智慧和体力。

Ming then told them how travel drastically changed with the invention of the automobile.

小明随后告诉他们，汽车发明以后，旅行的方式已彻底改变。

Lesson Five Calligraphy
第五课 书

As Ming wrote with black ink and a brush, he learned that Confucius's students were once taught calligraphy to temper their aggressiveness and arrogance.

小明用毛笔蘸墨写字，领悟到孔子的弟子们学习书法以戒骄戒躁。

Ming was able to find a pen from his backpack.

小明在他的背包里找到一支钢笔。

Lesson Six Mathematics
第六课 数

In the last lesson, Confucius showed Ming how mathematics could strengthen someone's mental quickness and sharpness.

在最后一课中，孔子告诉小明，数学可以强化人脑的反应速度和敏锐度。

Ming gave examples of things people use today to solve math problems like calculators.

小明介绍说今天的人们用计算器一类的东西来解决数学问题。

Men who excelled in these six arts were thought to have reached the state of perfection, Confucius said. To remember the lessons, Ming took many pictures while he was studying.

精通六艺的人被认为是完美的，孔子说。小明一边学习，一边照相，以免忘记所学内容。

Confucius and his students were amazed by the images his camera could capture.

孔子和他的弟子们觉得照相机能捕捉图像太不可思议了。

Ming could hardly believe it, but the day was coming to an end. After all the studying, he fell asleep on a go board.

不知不觉，天就黑了。学了那么多，小明趴在棋盘上睡着了。

When he woke up, Ming found himself back in the garden of the Kong Family Mansion. Then he noticed that his parents were waving to him. He couldn't wait to surprise them with his new knowledge.

醒来的时候，小明发现自己回到了孔府的花园，他看见爸爸妈妈正在朝他招手呢。他迫不及待地要用自己新学到的知识给他们一个惊喜。

Cultural Explanation
知识点

Main Gate (Temple of Confucius)
孔庙大门

Bixi that carrying the stone tablet (Temple of Confucius)
孔庙碑座赑屃

Dacheng Hall (Temple of Confucius)
孔庙大成殿

Apricot Pavilion (Temple of Confucius)
孔庙杏坛

Thirteen pavilions for sheltering imperial stone tablets (Temple of Confucius)
孔庙十三碑亭

Stone statues of Confucius's students (Cemetery of Confucius)
孔林石像生

The Analects 《论语》

The Analects records the words of Confucius and his disciples.
《论语》记录了孔子及其弟子言行。

三人行，
必有我师焉。

Where there are three together, one must be my teacher.

—The Analects

知之为知之，
不知为不知，
是智也。

Knowing is knowing and not knowing is not knowing, that is wisdom.

—The Analects